# Prince Noah

## and the School Pirates

**Silke Schnee**

Illustrated by Heike Sistig

Translated by Erna Albertz

**Plough Publishing House**

Published by Plough Publishing House
Walden, New York
Robertsbridge, England
Elsmore, Australia
www.plough.com

The German original edition of this book has been published under the
title *Prinz Seltsam und die Schulpiraten* by Neufeld Verlag, Schwarzenfeld, Germany.
Copyright ©2013 Neufeld Verlag. All rights reserved.

Illustrated by Heike Sistig
Translated and adapted from the German by Erna Albertz

ISBN: 978-0-87486-765-7
20 19 18 17 16   1 2 3 4 5 6

Library of Congress Cataloging-in-Publication Data pending.
Prince Noah and the School Pirates
Library of Congress Cataloging in Publication Control Number: 2016011233

Printed in Mexico

One day, Prince Noah wandered into the castle kitchen.

"Oh good," said the cook, "You can help me crack the eggs for a big chocolate cake!"

Prince Noah cracked one egg after another. Seven eggs landed in the bowl. Three slithered across the counter. Hmm, seven in the bowl – that number was clearly more than the three on the counter.

Noah's big brothers, Prince Luke and Prince Jonas, and his parents, the king and queen, heard Noah working out the numbers.

"Someone who can do so much belongs in school!" said the king. They all nodded proudly.

· · · · ·

In those long-ago days, children did not go to school in buildings but on majestic sailing ships. There was a ship for girls and one for boys, a ship for children with eye patches, a ship for children who had only one leg, and a ship for children who didn't learn so fast. No one knew why there were so many different ships, but it had always been that way.

The first day of school finally arrived. The sun had polished each and every one of its rays for this special day, and shone down on the colorfully decorated sailing ships from a cloudless blue sky. The ships rocked gently in the harbor. Then the royal trumpeters played a fanfare. Prince Noah started to dance for joy.

The children formed long lines and began to board their ships. The girls climbed aboard their pink ship while the boys clambered onto their orange one. The children who couldn't see well boarded a ship with high railings, and those who had trouble walking boarded one without stairs. Prince Noah got onto a multicolored ship which looked a little different from the others.

When all the children were safely aboard, a second fanfare sounded and they began their journey out onto the wild, wide sea. The parents waved and waved. Some of them had tears in their eyes. The queen sobbed and sniffed. The children waved back, and a few of them wiped their noses on their nice, clean school clothes because they felt quite small and alone.

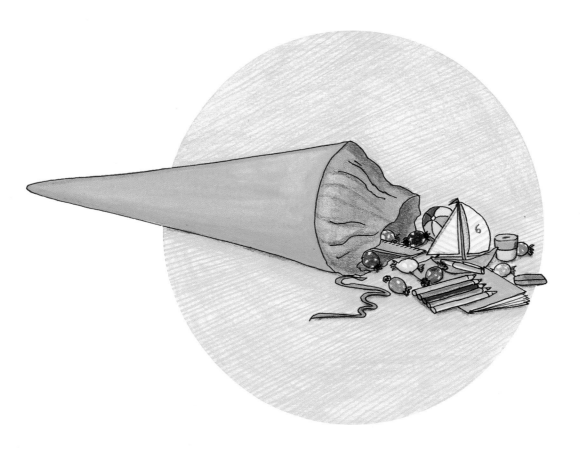

After a good night's sleep, the children began their lessons. "This is an A," said Miss Readmore, the teacher.

"A, A, A," answered Prince Noah loudly and clearly, while the whole class giggled and applauded. "An A, an A, an A!" sang Prince Noah, jumping on his desk. His friend John joined him in a wild dance. The class began to clap more loudly, and some children tapped their rulers against their desks and stamped a rhythm with their feet.

"A, A, A," they all screamed while Prince Noah performed the most amazing dance moves.

"Enough!" shouted Miss Readmore. "Sit down! Now you know the letter A, but who knows what five plus five is?"

"Two," answered Prince Noah.

"Wrong," said Miss Readmore.

"Not wrong," replied Prince Noah, holding up the five fingers on his right hand and then the five on his left. "Five and five makes two – hands!"

"Well," said Miss Readmore, "I'll have to think about that."

The first day of school was over. Prince Noah was mighty proud of himself.

Meanwhile, on their ship, the girls spent their days painting, embroidering, weaving, and knitting.

"But I also want to learn math!" exclaimed Maya. "It's so boring just doing handwork!"

Mrs. Chat, her teacher, hardly listened. Math had never been taught to girls. Back in those days, teachers thought it was much too complicated for them.

Maya found a nice piece of cloth and some shiny beads. First she sewed three beads in a row. Then she sewed another row below it. Then she sewed three more beads in a third row.

"Three plus three, plus three makes nine," she counted under her breath. She kept sewing rows of three until she had ten rows.

"Ten times three is thirty," she murmured, and was very pleased because she had figured out the answer without counting the beads.

"Why do people think math is so hard?" she wondered.

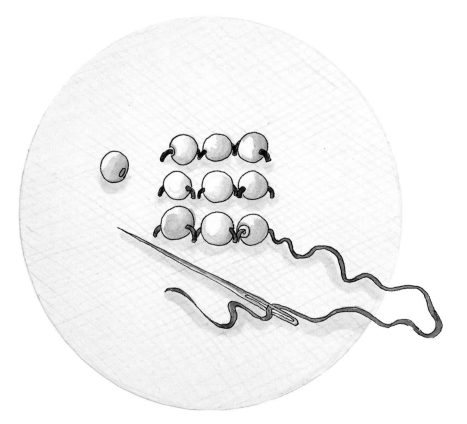

On the big ship for boys there was a constant ruckus. It sometimes smelled like sweat and dirty feet. The boys loved diving from the railing, swimming, climbing the ropes, fencing, and of course playing soccer.

Prince Jonas had just shot another of his famous penalty kicks.

"Hooray!" cheered his friend Leo. "And now a center kick to me!" The ball crashed into a cabinet, barely missed a lamp overhead, and smashed straight through a glass porthole into the ocean.

"Awesome shot!" yelled Leo, "And now we need a new ball!"

"How will I ever turn these young rascals into respectable gentlemen?" sighed their teacher, Mr. Proper. He had long since given up trying to teach the boys anything except climbing, diving, and playing soccer.

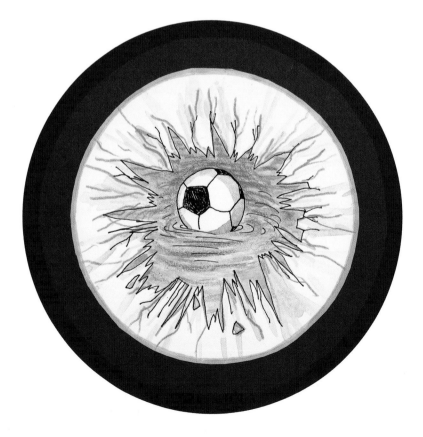

On the ship for the boys and girls with one leg it was much quieter. In the mornings, they learned to read and write, but their afternoons were often quite boring.

It was so boring that one day a boy called Max started carving deep notches in his wooden leg. Every day he carved a new notch. After four weeks he had made twenty-eight notches, one next to the other, just like the sharp teeth of a shark.

· · · · ·

The ship for children with eye patches was even quieter. Those who could see with one eye and those who could not see at all worked mostly with their hands, forming letters out of sand and seawater and leaving them to dry on the deck. Day by day, they slowly formed all the letters of the alphabet.

Because they could not trust their eyes, they were training their ears. They learned that the noises they heard could tell them whether the water was choppy or calm, whether it was day or night, and whether a room had a high or a low ceiling. Their ears became as sensitive as those of bats, and they were amazed at how many sounds they could recognize.

"What's that?" cried Anton, one of the blind boys. "I hear something floating toward us." He felt for a net and lowered it into the water.

Soon he felt a tug in the net. He quickly pulled it out of the water and heaved it on board. What had he caught? A soccer ball!

The sun came up and the sun went down. One day followed the next, and the children were beginning to wish for the holidays, when they would be back on land with their families.

One day Anton was sitting quietly on deck when he remarked, "A storm is coming; I feel a change in the air!"

But the sun was still shining, so no one believed him.

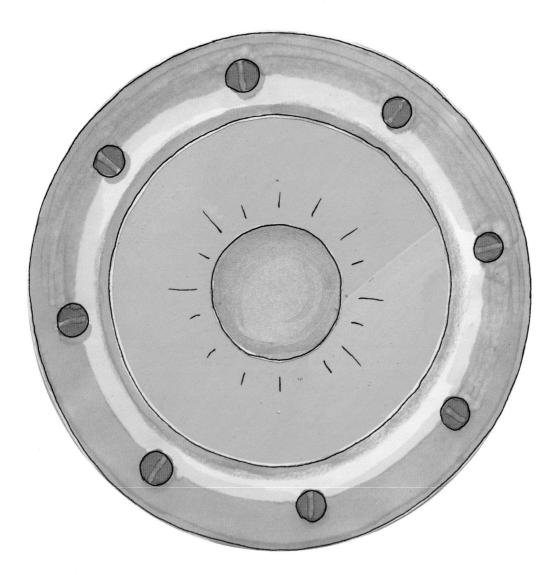

Suddenly, however, the sky turned dark, rain started to fall, and the waves grew higher. The wind picked up and the ships began to rock.

"All hands below deck," the teachers shouted. The storm broke just as they were fastening down the last hatches. Thunder and lightning filled the air. Waves crashed over the decks and a howling wind tore at the sails. The ships danced like walnut shells on the wild ocean. All night long the terrible storm raged, and it was morning before the teachers dared go on deck.

"Help!" they cried when they looked at their compass and charts. "We've been driven far off course – we are now in pirate waters! Quick, quick – away from here!"

But it was already too late. On the horizon they saw an enormous, frightful pirate ship barreling straight toward them, carrying forty wicked pirates who were all eagerly awaiting their captain's command.

"Storm the ships!" Captain Redbeard cried.

Before anyone could think, the pirates had taken command of all five ships. They bound the children and threw them in the pirate ship's hold, then made straight for the pirate island. As soon as they dropped anchor, the pirates chased the children up into a prison tower. There they sat, shivering and shaking on the straw that covered the floor, wrapping their arms around each other for comfort.

Suddenly the door opened. "Here is some bread and water. Eat this and go to sleep!" shouted Captain Redbeard. Then he slammed the door and slid a heavy board across the outside so no one could escape.

Through a tiny window high in the tower, the good moon shone down on the children. Some of them wept quietly.

"We have to figure out how to get out of here," whispered Prince Luke.

"How can we?" asked Prince Jonas quietly. "The door is locked and barred, and the window up there is blocked by wooden bars!"

"I think I have an idea," said Max after a while. Everyone looked at him in amazement. How could a boy with a wooden leg help?

"You could use my leg as a saw!" Max said, as he started to take off his leg with the shark-tooth notches. A murmur went through the crowd.

"Excellent plan," exclaimed Prince Jonas. "Now all we have to do is get up to that window."

"And down the other side," declared Maya. "I counted the steps as we were being led up here. There are thirty-five, and each is about two hands high. We'll have to braid a rope seventy hands long from this straw. If everyone helps, we can do it."

Everyone stared at Maya. The boys were especially impressed.

"Fantastic," said Prince Luke. "Can you make a team, and start to braid right away? Everyone else who can, make a pyramid under the window. I will climb up and saw through the bars."

"Stop, stop!" whispered Anton excitedly, "That will be much too loud. I can hear the breathing of the two pirates who are sitting just outside the door."

Horrified, they all sat down. Anton was right. The guards would hear them sawing through the bars, and their escape would fail. Time passed. The tower clock struck midnight. All was quiet.

Suddenly Prince Noah jumped up. "A, A, A," he sang as loudly as he could, dancing and furiously waving his arms. John immediately joined him, and all the girls and boys from his class jumped up, clapping and stamping.

"What's going on?" yelled the guards, opening the door. "Stop that immediately!"

But Prince Noah only sang more loudly and danced more wildly than before. The whole class followed his lead, clapping and stamping faster and faster.

The guards looked frightened. "The children have gone crazy!" said one. "Let's leave them alone!" said the other. And as fast as they had come, they disappeared, slamming the door and barring it behind them.

"Come on, let's dance!" called out Prince Noah. Everybody knew right away what he was up to.

Quickly, the boys built a pyramid. Prince Luke climbed up with Max's wooden leg and began to saw. The girls began braiding straw as fast as they could. Prince Noah and John danced and sang until they were exhausted, while all their classmates and the children with eye patches clapped and stamped.

Just as the moon was going down and the sun was beginning to rise, Prince Luke sawed through the last bar.

"Quick, before the guards come back," urged Prince Luke, fastening the straw rope to the stump of one of the bars. "Each of you bigger boys and girls, carry a younger one and climb up the pyramid to me."

Without a moment's hesitation, the children began to climb up to the window and let themselves down the rope on the outside. They quietly and carefully helped each other, whispering words of encouragement. Finally, only Prince Jonas and Leo were left in the tower cell. Leo tried standing on Prince Jonas's shoulders, but he couldn't quite reach up to Prince Luke, who was still balanced on the window sill. What were they to do? Aha! They took off their pants and tossed them up to Prince Luke, who made a rope by knotting the pant legs together, and lowered it down so they could scramble up to freedom.

When all the children had safely arrived on the rocky ground outside the tower, Prince Noah looked around. "Hooray, hooray, hooray, the pirate ship has gone away!" he exclaimed. Sure enough, no ship was in sight – only water far and wide.

"But how will we ever get home?" one of the smallest children cried.

"Shhh!" whispered Anton. "I can hear something that sounds like water lapping against a ship's hull. Over there." He pointed toward the middle of the island.

"Well then, let's go!" said Prince Luke, who did not for a moment doubt that Anton had heard right. After they had walked a little way, they came to a small, hidden cove. And there, concealed behind a grove of palms, was the colorful ship on which Noah had learned about the letter A. There were no pirates to be seen – the ship had been left unguarded.

"Hurry, we have to get out of here before the pirates return!" said Prince Jonas. Cautiously, the children helped one another climb down the rocks and onto the ship.

There they found their teachers tied to the main mast. With nimble fingers, the children untied the ropes. Before they had time to tell of their adventures, Prince Luke gave the order: "Set sail! Full speed ahead!" Prince Noah and his friends danced for joy.

Quickly, the ship set sail and before the sun had reached its highest point in the sky, they were safely out of the pirates' reach. They sang, danced, and celebrated far into the night, then fell exhausted into their berths.

A loud gong woke them from blissful sleep. "Wake up!" shouted Miss Readmore. "It's lesson time!"

Since there was only one ship now, the children had to have their lessons all together. And do you know what? That worked out very well: Maya helped the boys with math, and they showed her and all the other girls how to dive, fence, and, of course, play soccer. Anton borrowed Max's leg for math, because he could easily count the notches to find out what three plus three would come to.

Sometimes, when everyone was very quiet, Anton guided them through the world of sounds. Then the beating of waves would tickle their ears, and a change in the air could give them goosebumps.

No one was ever bored again.

Prince Noah was happy to be with his brothers and all the other children. Now they could laugh and learn and live together. Their journey home was much more fun and everyone learned a lot. Soon the coast of their homeland came into sight.

Their parents were already waiting at the shore – a little worried but also excited. They hugged their children, happy to have them home safely. Then everyone celebrated a great homecoming festival under the golden sun and the deep blue sky.

Prince Noah beamed as he raised his hands and began to dance. And if he hasn't stopped dancing yet, he is dancing still.

## The Author

Silke Schnee is a journalist and works as a television producer for a public broadcaster in Cologne, Germany. She is married and has three

sons. Her youngest son Noah was born in July 2008 with Trisomy 21 (Down syndrome). She writes, "At first when Noah was born, we were shocked and sad. The catalyst for this book was witnessing the effect he had on many people, despite being categorized as disabled. In fact, our little prince brings much love, joy, and sunshine not only to us, but to all around him. Children are a wonder, and we must see them with the eyes of our heart – each child just the way he or she is."

Bild: © WDR

## The Illustrator

Heike Sistig studied special education and art and is a trained art therapist. She works as an editor for children's television programming. She has illus-

trated several children's books, and has exhibited her collages in several art galleries. She lives with her family in Cologne, Germany.

## Like a Fairytale?

My husband is not a king, and I am no queen – but we do have three real-life princes: Luke, Jonas, and Noah, who appear under their real names

in my books *The Prince Who Was Just Himself* and *Prince Noah and the School Pirates*.

Prince Noah, the little blond boy in the middle of this family photo, is blessed with an extra chromosome. Noah laughs a lot. He also smears spaghetti sauce in his hair, throws laundry into the toilet, and tries to discover what garden slugs taste like, perhaps mistaking them for Tootsie Rolls.

Our daily life as a noisy, ragtag, "special needs" family is certainly no fairy tale. I sometimes wish that our society – like the characters in my books – would proclaim: "Three cheers for Noah! A sunshine who shows us how beautiful life can be, who proves that higher, faster, and better are not necessarily the most important goals! Noah, the one who makes our happiness complete!"

I know, that's probably asking too much. It would be enough if Noah could attend the "normal" elementary school in our district, something that is still not taken for granted here in Germany. It would be enough if I could do less fighting against the prejudices that pigeonhole children like Noah. Yes, our daily reality is far removed from the magic of a fairy tale.

And yet there are so many magical days. Days in which Noah shows us the craziest dance moves and gives the most beautiful kisses; or our three princes chase each other around the yard, bubbling over with spring fever; or the neighbors' lovely daughter claims that Noah is the sweetest and smartest boy on the whole street.

Then I wonder, "Is there anything more beautiful on earth than the love of such little people? Is there anything more meaningful than teaching my son how to put on his shoes by himself? What could touch my heart more deeply than the sight of my slumbering child with his little thumb in his mouth?" At such moments my life indeed seems like a fairy tale.

—Silke Schnee

AR Level _____ Lexile _____

AR Pts. _____ RC Pts._____